J PAR STORYTIME KIT REP 2

Reptiles: snap, slither & slime [storytime kit]
Total - 12 pieces
31112018411179

Leon
the Chameleon

To Ernesto, my best friend and Leon's greatest supporter.
Special thanks to Michèle Lemieux for her guidance and inspiration.

Text and illustrations © 2001 Mélanie Watt

Kids Can Press acknowledges the financial support of the Ontario Arts Council,
the Canada Council for the Arts and the Government of Canada, through
the BPIDP, for our publishing activity.

Published in Canada by
Kids Can Press Ltd.
25 Dockside Drive
Toronto, ON M5A 0B5

Published in the U.S. by
Kids Can Press Ltd.
2250 Military Road
Tonawanda, NY 14150

www.kidscanpress.com

The artwork in this book was rendered in acrylic and black ink.
The text is set in Stone Sans.

Edited by Debbie Rogosin
Designed by Julia Naimska

The hardcover edition of this book is smyth sewn casebound.
The paperback edition of this book is limp sewn with a drawn-on cover.
Manufactured in Tseung Kwan O, NT Hong Kong, China, in 12/2010 by
Paramount Printing Co. Ltd.

CM 01 0 9 8 7 6 5 4 3 2
CM PA 03 0 9 8 7 6 5 4

National Library of Canada Cataloguing in Publication Data

Watt, Mélanie, 1975–
    Leon the chameleon

ISBN 978-1-55074-867-3 (bound)   ISBN 978-1-55337-527-2 (pbk.)

1. Color — Juvenile literature. I. Title.

QC495.5.W38 2001   j535.6   C00-932106-3

Kids Can Press is a *Corus*™ Entertainment company

Leon
the Chameleon

Mélanie Watt

Kids Can Press

Leon the chameleon was different from all the other chameleons.
When the others sat on a green leaf, they turned green.
When they stood on yellow sand, they turned yellow.
And when they swam in the blue pond, they turned blue.

But not Leon. When Leon sat on a green leaf, he turned red.

When Leon stood on yellow sand, he turned purple.

And when Leon swam in the blue pond, he turned orange.

Leon didn't do this on purpose. He wanted to be the same as the other chameleons.

He just couldn't help turning the opposite color.

Sometimes being different made Leon feel frightened.
He couldn't camouflage himself when there was danger.

Sometimes being different made Leon feel embarrassed.
He always stood out in a crowd.

Sometimes being different made Leon feel lonely.

He didn't join the other little chameleons because he felt that he didn't fit in.

Leon thought there was no place for him in the group, especially when the others played their favorite game — camouflage and seek.

One day, the little chameleons decided to go exploring.
Leon was curious. So he followed them out of the forest,
trying his best to stay hidden.

The little chameleons walked for a long time.
After a while, they realized that they were lost.
The little chameleons were scared.
Leon was scared, too.

Leon huddled behind a rock until he couldn't stand being alone any longer.

He peeked out, and the little chameleons spotted him immediately.

To Leon's amazement, they were happy to see him.

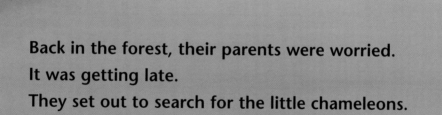

Back in the forest, their parents were worried.
It was getting late.
They set out to search for the little chameleons.

Their parents walked for a long time.
But there was no sign of the little chameleons.
Then, far off in the distance, they saw a green dot.

It was Leon!
Thanks to his color, the little chameleons
had been found, safe and sound.
Everyone was overjoyed.

After a day full of adventure, the chameleons returned home. This time, Leon walked with all the others. He was still the opposite color, but now he had his own special place in the group. This time, being different made Leon feel proud.

Did you know?

Red, yellow and blue are primary colors.
They are the three most important colors.

When these colors are mixed, we get
three new colors.
Red mixed with yellow gives orange.
Yellow mixed with blue gives green.
Blue mixed with red gives purple.
Mixing the six colors together gives black.

The complementary or contrasting color is always
found at the opposite side of the color circle.
Red is the complementary color of green.
Yellow is the complementary color of purple.
Blue is the complementary color of orange.

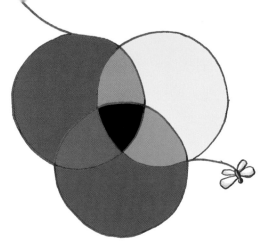